Robots Everywhere

Denny Hebson

Illustrations by Todd Hoffman

WALKER & COMPANY
NEW YORK

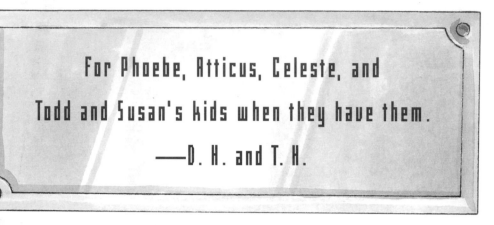

For Phoebe, Atticus, Celeste, and
Todd and Susan's kids when they have them.
—D. H. and T. H.

Text copyright © 2004 by Dennis Hebson
Illustrations copyright © 2004 by Todd Hoffman

First published in the United States of America in 2004 by Walker Publishing Company, Inc.

Published simultaneously in Canada by Fitzhenry and Whiteside, Markham, Ontario L3R 4T8

For information about permission to reproduce selections from
this book, write to Permissions, Walker & Company, 104 Fifth Avenue, New York, New York 10011

Library of Congress Cataloging-in-Publication Data
Hebson, Dennis.
Robots everywhere / Dennis Hebson ; illustrations by Todd Hoffman.
p. cm.
Summary: Various kinds of robots go about their daily activities, such as riding buses, rusting at the beach, and eating metal nuts.
ISBN 0-8027-8892-0 — ISBN 0-8027-8893-9 (rein)
[1. Robots—Fiction. 2. Stories in rhyme.] I. Hoffman, Todd, ill. II. Title.
PZ8.3.H3839Ro 2004
[E]—dc21   2003050088

The artist used Dr. Martin inks on Canson cold press watercolor paper (grain finish) to create the illustrations for this book.

Book design by Victoria Allen

Visit Walker & Company's Web site at www.walkeryoungreaders.com

Printed in Hong Kong

2 4 6 8 10 9 7 5 3 1

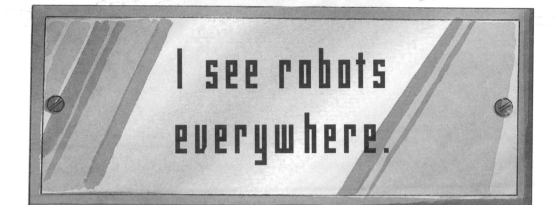

I see robots everywhere.

With metal shoes

and springs for hair.

Playing catch with
sewer grates.

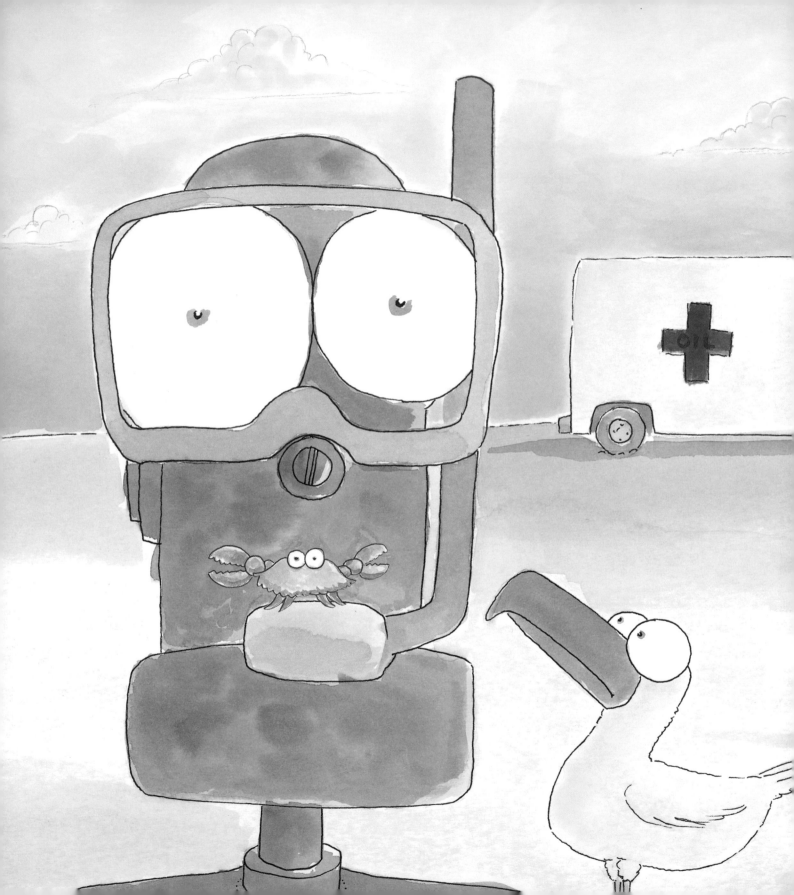

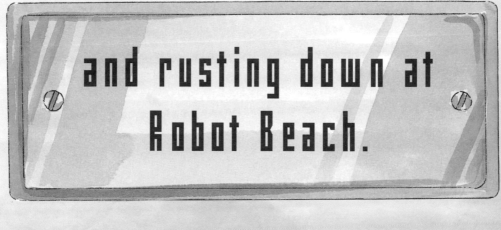

and rusting down at Robot Beach.

Sleeping under sheets of foil.

Filing nails,

For Maya

Library of Congress Cataloging-in-Publication Data available.
ISBN 978-1-4521-5527-2
Manufactured in China.

MIX
Paper from
responsible sources
FSC
www.fsc.org   FSC™ C104723

Design by Sara Gillingham Studio. Typeset in Austral Slab Rough.
The illustrations in this book were made with pencil,
watercolor, ink, vintage book paper, and an iMac.

10 9 8 7 6 5 4 3 2 1

Chronicle Books LLC, 680 Second Street, San Francisco, California 94107

Chronicle Books—we see things differently.
Become part of our community at www.chroniclekids.com.

MABEL
A MERMAID FABLE

Rowboat Watkins

chronicle books · san francisco

What was weird about Mabel wasn't her mustache.

Her dad had a mustache.

Her mom had a mustache.

Her big sisters had matching mustaches.

Even her baby brother had a tiny baby mustache.

What was weird about Mabel was
that she had no mustache at all.

Mabel tried hiding her nose
behind jaunty shells

and by wearing
seaweed falsies,

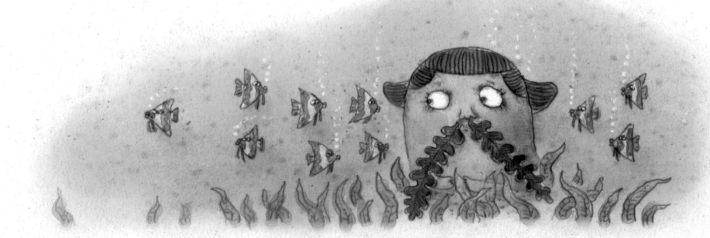

Mabel had no idea what a nudibranch was, but if she WAS one the only thing to do was . . .

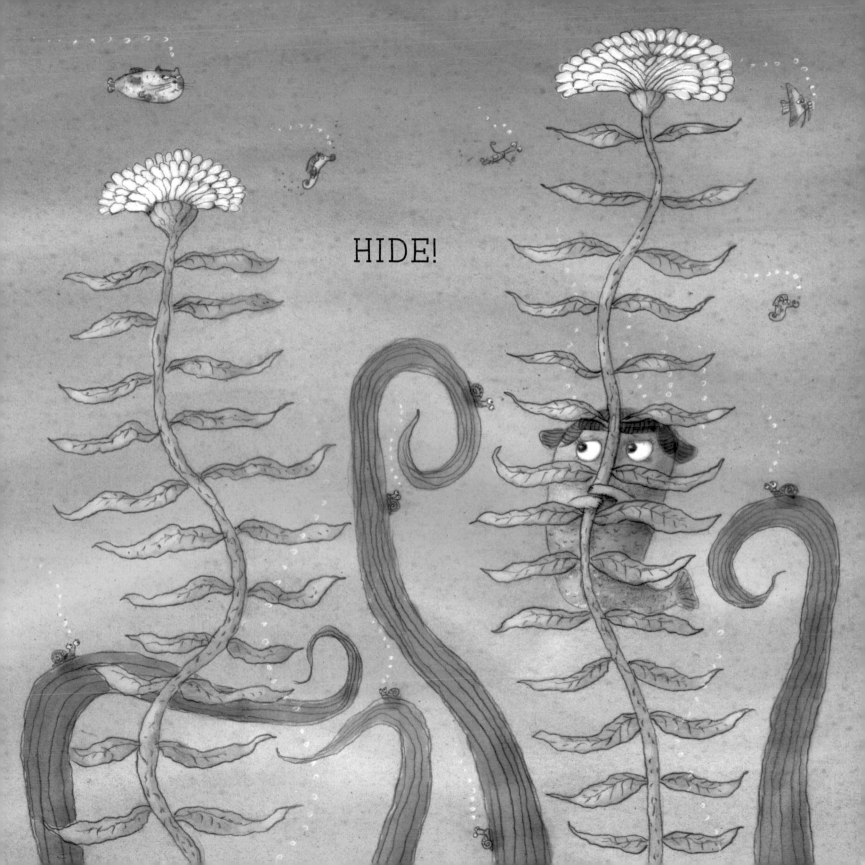

HIDE!

So she frittered away 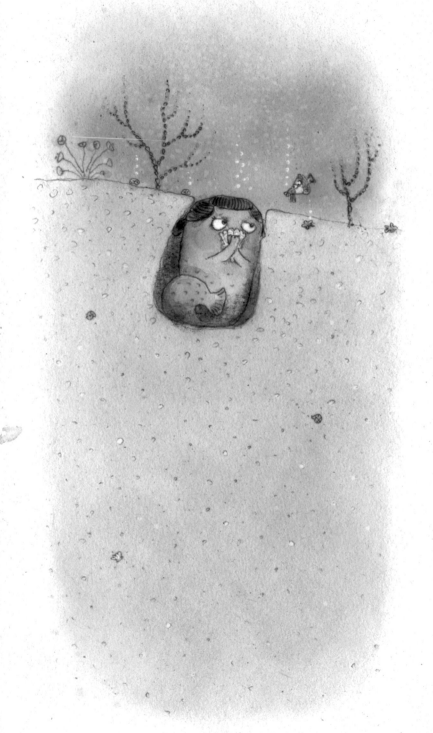 who knows how long,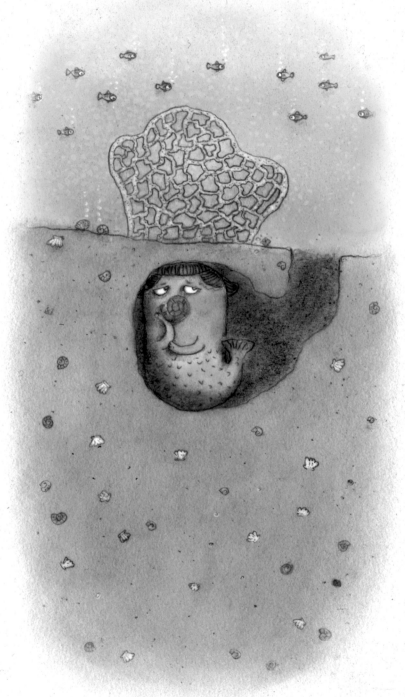

hiding in holes

along the ocean floor.

"Why are you here?"
Mabel asked.

"Because I only
have seven legs."

"That sure sounds
like a lot of legs."

"I'm supposed to have eight," said Lucky.

"What can you do with eight legs
that you can't do with seven?" Mabel asked.

"Count to eight," said Lucky.

"I can teach you to count to eight!" said Mabel.

Mabel actually helped Lucky count all the way up to . . .

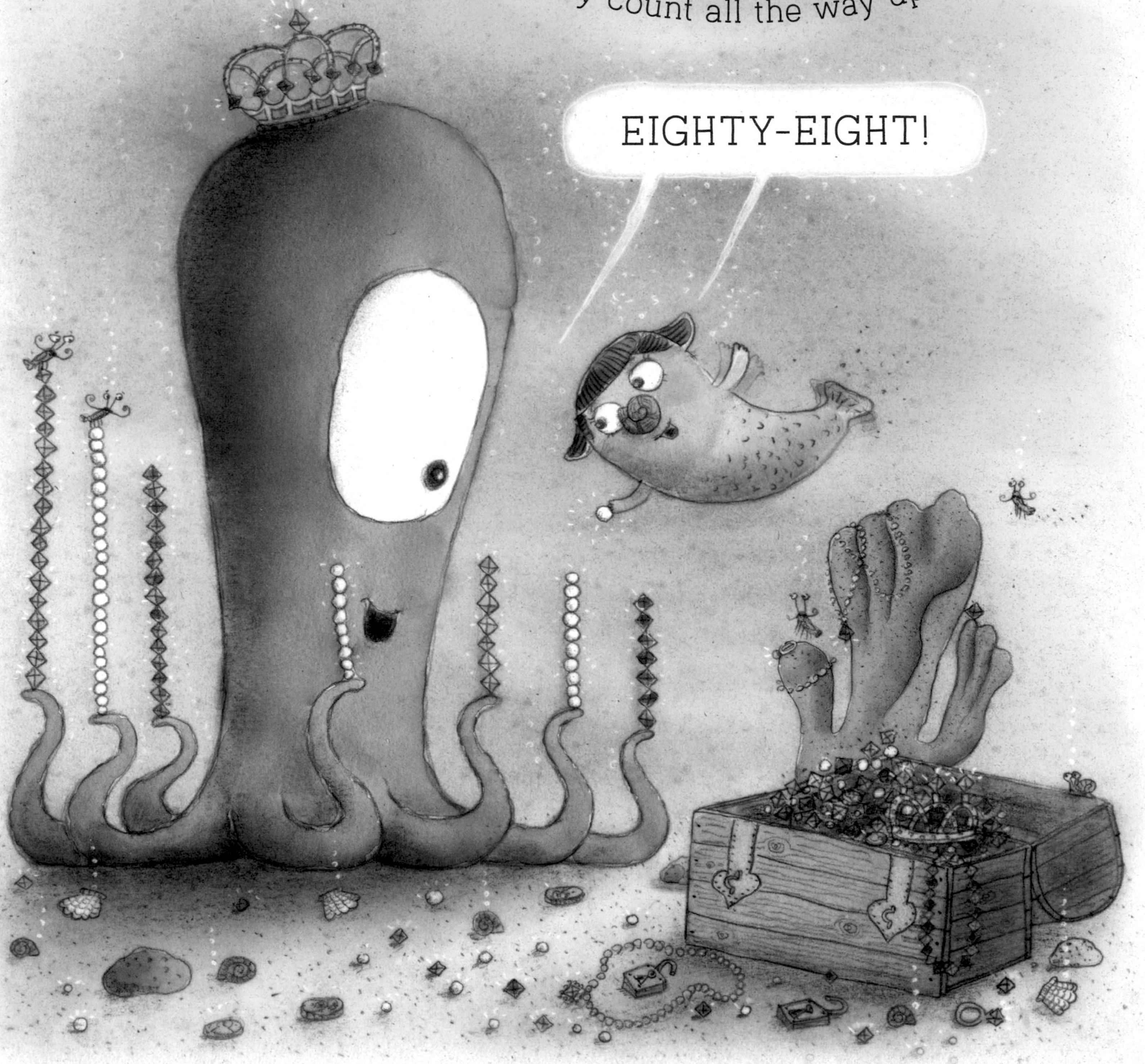

And Lucky sort of taught Mabel how to juggle.

GREAT!

Then they pretended to be King and Queen of the Corals.

NUDIBR

"Sorry," said Lucky. "I leak when I'm scared."

"That's ok," said Mabel. "What's a nudibranch?"

"Nudibranchs are sea slugs," said Lucky.

"Oh," said Mabel. "So that's why they're awful."

"They aren't awful, silly," said Lucky.

"Nudibranchs are . . ."

I'm
amazing?

Suddenly,

Mabel realized

everything she ever

really needed . . .

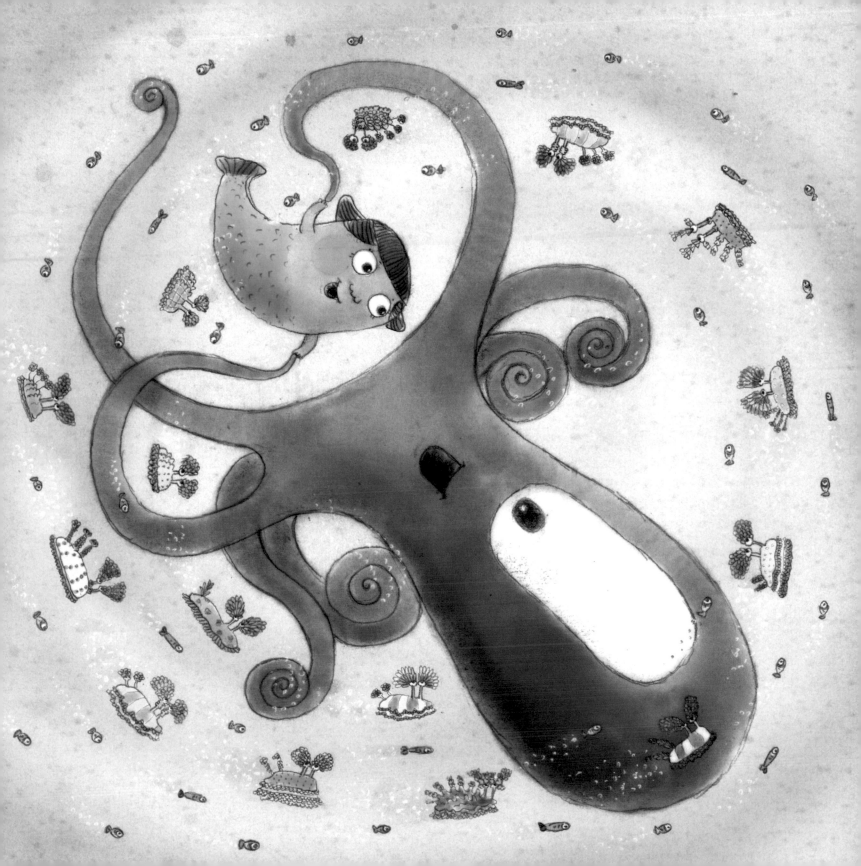

was already right under her nose.

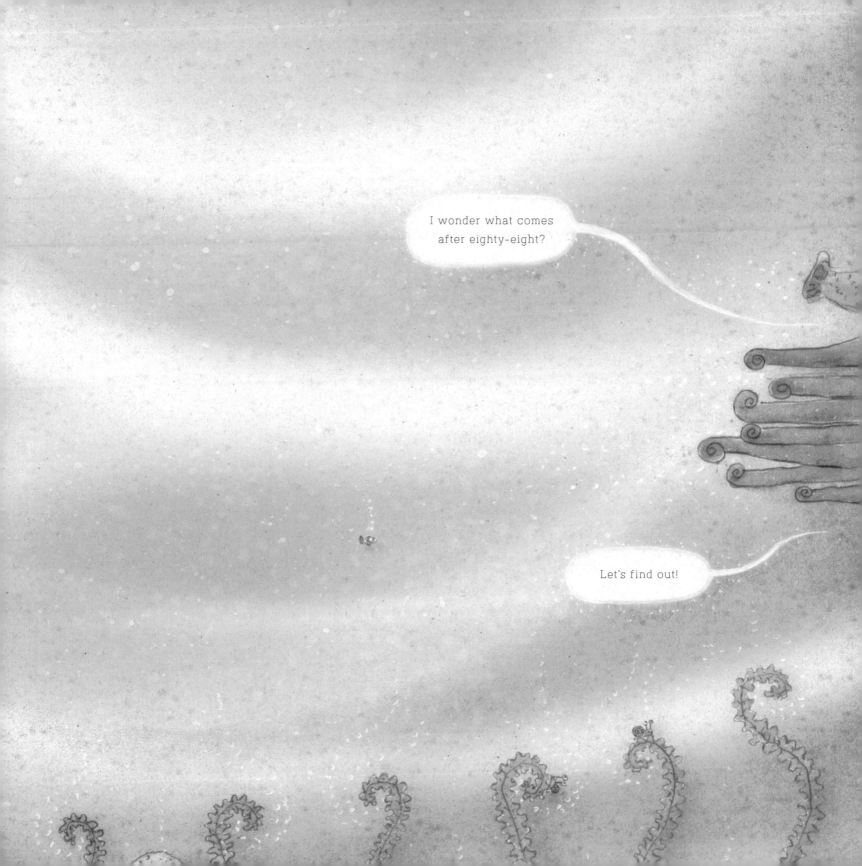